The Passion of Roger
Sophie MacDonald
Copyright Sophie MacDonald 2013
Published at Smashwords

Share your thoughts with us.
Take a moment to tell us how we're doing. Your feedback really matters.

You can reach us by:
Email: *my777books@yahoo.com*

Search for other titles by Sophie MacDonald.

The Passion of Roger

CHAPTER 1

One summer day, young Teddy Lake was walking home after shooting hoops at the schoolyard with some friends. As he opened the front door and entered his house he noticed something peculiar. The house was very quiet. This was unusual since his mom, Sandy, usually had the TV on watching her soaps, or was on the phone with one of her friends. The house was so quiet that Teddy felt like calling out for his mom. Then he thought he heard something. It sounded like a moan when someone is delighting on chocolate. It was coming from his parent's bedroom. As he crept closer to the doorway, Teddy heard a woman's voice and the sound of smacking lips. His mom? He also heard another moan and a guy's voice say "Oh yeah!" What the hell was going on?

As Teddy peeked around the corner of the doorway he saw an incredible sight. There was his mom, naked on her bed, on her knees, her face hovering over a guy's cock. And not just any guy, either. It was James, Teddy's friend from school. The young man was lying on his parents' bed, his hands holding Sandy's head as she gave the young man a blow job.

Teddy was shocked. No wonder James didn't feel like shooting hoops today, Teddy thought. Instead, James was getting his cock serviced by Ted's mom! The older woman's wavy blond hair fell around the young cock. She sucked the cockhead, swirling her tongue around it, lowering her head down over the length taking more and more of the shaft down her throat.

"Oh, fuck yeah," James moaned. Ted was stunned and his knees grew weak beneath him as he watched his mother's mouth stretch oh-so wide and lower itself to the base of his friend's cock. When Sandy's nose nestled in James' sparsely-haired crotch, Ted's eyes grew even wider. "Is his cock...all the way down her throat?" he wondered. Then Sandy slowly raised her head leaving a trail of saliva coating the young shaft. Her lips were once again circling the cockhead, and then she removed it from her mouth.

"Wow!" Teddy thought, looking at James' saliva-coated cock. Teddy's young cock, when hard was maybe five inches and not very thick, but James cock looked ridiculous on his wiry frame. It was long but also thick, and Teddy realized immediately what his mom liked. Sandy kissed and licked the cock some more and then changed positions so that her ass was now facing Teddy. He'd never seen his mother's ass before and here he was staring not only at her creamy asscheeks but Teddy could also see her pussy, drawn outward, and very, very wet. Teddy continued to stare at his mom's ass. It really looked good.

Meanwhile, as Sandy held James' cock with one hand, she began to suck on it again. With her free hand, Sandy began playing with her cunt; rubbing her clit, inserting her fingers inside to fuck herself. Then James moved his left hand to Sandy's ass, felt her asscheeks, and inserted his finger inside her asshole! They both finger-fucked Sandy's cunt and ass as she sucked James cock. Teddy watched intently, breathing heavily as their fingers worked in and out of his mom's holes.

"I gotta have you!" Sandy exclaimed, taking the large cock out of her mouth. She then got up on the bed, straddled James' cock and lowered her aching cunt down over the hard, young shaft. Sandy began humping up and down, fucking James' cock as he held her. He then pulled her to him to suck on her erect nipples as Sandy tried to fuck his cock at the same time.

"Oh, god, I need this!" Sandy cried, and with that she backed away from James nursing on her, and started frantically fucking his prick.

"Oh! Oh! Oh! Oh! Oh!" she cried. Watching from his hideaway, Teddy's mouth was wide open. Was this really his own mom? He watched her breasts flop up and down, her nipples so hard and long, with his friend's saliva now flying off them. And then there was James. Moaning and groaning beneath her saying something like "gonna cum." Sandy quickly got off the huge, slick teen cock and started fisting it, crying out "Yes! Come on! Cum! Cum on me!" James then let out a loud cry and shot a gallon of semen straight into his buddies' mom's face. "Yes!" Sandy cried.

"Oh god yeah!" James cried with her. Stream after stream of semen shot out of his cock onto Sandy's face, her hair, and dripping down onto her tits.

She was soaked! Teddy was shocked. When he would fist himself, his cum only dribbled out. Exhausted, James' head swayed back and forth on the pillow. Teddy's father's pillow, he noticed. Meanwhile, his mom was scooping up all the cum she could and fed it to her hungry mouth, moaning with each finger full. "How was that?" Sandy asked the young stud with a smile.

"Great," he moaned.

"Better than last time?" she asked. "Last time?" Teddy thought. "Fuck, when did they do this before?" he thought. "How often?"

"Yeah, it's always great," James replied. "Always?" Teddy thought. He was totally stunned by all that was happening before his eyes. After making some small talk for a minute, James spoke up. "Would you do something for me?"

"What?" she asked stroking his virile young cock back to life.

"Well, my kid brother is at that age, you know, and he's always talking about girls and stuff and -"

"Is he a virgin?"

"Uh, yeah. I mean would you mind?"

"Taking his virginity? Not at all! I took yours didn't I?"

"Great! When can we -"

"I don't know but I'll let you know. As usual with us, just be patient. And keep him away from girls his own age! I want that virgin flesh all to myself!"

"I will," James said with a laugh.

"And then after we get through with your brother - what's his name?"

"Jason."

"After I help out Jason maybe you can do ME a favor."

"What?"

Lying on her side of the bed Sandy spread her legs and said, "Come fuck my hot, horny cunt with your huge cock and I'll whisper it in your ear, you nasty boy!"

James quickly got up and the sight made Teddy back away from the door in fear. When he heard his mom yell out in pleasure, Teddy quickly took a peek inside. There, James was on top of his mom, pounding his thick cock inside her cunt. They both moaned and cried in pleasure as Sandy's cunt made these squishy noises.

"Fuck me! Oh god, Fuck me!" Sandy cried, her face contorted, eyes gleaming. "Oh, yeah! Oh! I love your big teenage cock in my mother-whore cunt!"

It was all too much for Teddy as he quietly crept down the hall and flew out the front door. When he was halfway down the block only then did he notice how uncomfortable he felt. His own cock was straining in his shorts and he had this big wet stain at his crotch.

Teddy's life was permanently changed that day. From then on, he saw his mom not so much as "mom" but as "woman." He would often fantasize about her but never had the guts to actually go for it. He needn't have bothered. Sandy had already seen her son naked and hard by accident, while he masturbated, and while she was tempted to help her son relieve himself, she was afraid it might damage their relationship. What if he freaked out by the thought? Besides Sandy was hardly impressed with Teddy. "He's just like his father," she thought to herself.

One night when James was sleeping over, Sandy heard noise coming from their room around midnight. Getting up and leaving her snoring husband she walked down the hall and opened Teddy's door. Her eyes bulged and her mouth fell open. There, kneeling on the floor were Teddy and his friend, masturbating to a porn magazine. Sandy was shocked but when she noticed James' cock, her mouth grew dry. The forty year-old mother had needs. And fantasies. But James was too young! He was her son's friend! It wouldn't be right! But his cock was huge! Her husband was losing interest! He was so small! He never satisfied her! Oh, to try a big one, just once!

Two weeks later Sandy took James' virginity when he came around looking for Teddy with only Sandy at home. And months later Teddy learned their secret, which soon became his biggest fantasy. He wished to fuck his mom, too, but didn't think he had what she wanted. Teddy never knew if James' brother Jason was brought in to their sex-play, but he found himself fantasizing about his mom and James. It always made him hard and he whacked off countless times to the thought of them fucking. Before going off to college, Teddy caught his mom and friend in the throes of passion several times. One question that always nagged at him, then, as it did twenty-five years later. What were those "favors" his mom always asked of James when he caught them in bed? It was like a code term. If he'd only known. By the time Teddy had gone off to college, his mom had been gangbanged by Teddy's small circle of friends at least a dozen times, fulfilling Sandy's fantasies.

Among Teddy's friends, their best kept secret was what a slut his mom was!

Now twenty-five years later, a grown Ted was still fantasizing. As he surfed the Internet at home he found his favorite erotic stories site, Literotica. Printing out his favorite stories for his own private consumption, Ted's dreams never left him. They were just now altered a bit.

"Dinner's ready!" cried his wife. As Ted got up from his study, he entered the dining room as his lovely wife of nearly twenty years, Susan, placed food on the table. Just then their handsome, young son, Roger entered the room. "I'm starving!" he said.

As the family sat down to eat, Ted noticed his blond-haired, blue-eyed wife, who looked very much like his mom in her younger days. Then he looked at his handsome, well-built son. Ted had developed a new fantasy. And now was the time to put it into action.

CHAPTER 2

After dinner, Ted retired to his study, sat at his desk, turned on his computer, and logged-on, going straight to Literotica. He had his family convinced that he needed to work a lot at home, but the truth of the matter was that Ted hadn't really needed to do work at home for over two years. Technology had solved that dilemma. This was his quiet time; Lock the door, read his stories and jack off. Neither Susan or Roger ever figured it out. Tonight he found just what he was looking for, as he printed out two slightly different stories, each packing the punch he expected.

The first he folded up and put in an envelope. He addressed it to his son and typed up his name and address so he wouldn't make out Ted's handwriting. The second he held on to. Ted then logged off and walked out of the study. With Roger watching TV in the living room and Susan on the phone in the kitchen, Ted quietly made his way towards Roger's bathroom, with folded story in hand, knowing that Susan was going to do a wash the next day. Ted placed the story in Roger's hamper under a couple of shirts to be washed and then quickly walked out.

The following morning, Ted woke, showered and dressed as calmly as possible while his wife was making breakfast in the kitchen. After eating, Ted said goodbye to Roger and nervously kissed his wife goodbye and headed out the door. Driving to work he pulled over to drop the envelope containing the other story in the mailbox. Ted's plan was now complete. All that was left to do was wait for the fireworks.

Late that morning Susan went into her son's bathroom to get his clothes. As she made her way to the washing machine she sorted out the clothes but felt something funny.

"What is this?" she asked pulling out some folded paper. Susan unfolded it and looked at it. "What the..?" It was a story, it seemed. It was titled "Fucking my Mom," by someone or something called The Devil's Advocate.

Susan started to read the account of a young man who was constantly horny for his sexy mom. Then one day while his mom was in the shower, the son entered, scaring her half-to-death until she saw his huge, raging erection. Five minutes later the mother was leaning against the shower wall with her son's monster cock all the way up her cunt. "At last!" the story concluded. "I got to fuck my mom!"

Susan breathing heavily, nervously, leaned against the washing machine as it went into spin cycle. So did she. "Where did he get this?" Susan asked. She noticed the story came from the Internet. "Does Roger...want to...Oh my god!" As she walked away, she headed for the living room. Susan sat down on the couch, her hand covering her mouth. Then she got up and began pacing around the room, disbelieving. Her own teenage son wanted...to fuck his mother! "He wants me!" she thought.

At first Susan tried to rationalize it. "He's young. He's, well...horny. He has needs. He probably just masturbates to this stuff. Oh my god, he masturbates?" Susan pictured her baby, lying in bed reading this filth while his hand went up and down his big, long, thick - "god no, this is so wrong!" she thought. It actually hurt like hell. Susan had needs, too. She and Ted had sex maybe once a month, and he was hardly great. Besides his cock never satisfied her, but he was a good provider and she was sure he never fucked around. Susan had had an affair or two but that was a long time ago, and she was trying to remain faithful. It wasn't easy.

Her friend Donna who was always calling, wanted Susan to go out with her. Divorced two years now, Donna often called Susan to inform her of her exploits. Donna had celebrated her divorce by going out to a club and picking up two, horny nineteen year-old black guys. When she later told Susan of the double penetration she'd received, and the size of their cocks, the frustrated blond wife nearly had an orgasm. Susan had her own fantasies. If Ted only knew what was being discussed when Donna called, every so-often replaying her latest conquests with her young black studs.

"You know, Susan, just name the time and I'll invite them over, so you'll find out just what you've been missing," Donna once reminded her. "How big's Ted's cock again?" she teased. After reading the Mom-son story one more time, a frustrated, horny Susan retired to her bedroom, fell on her bed and cried. It had been so long since she'd been fucked real good. Twenty minutes later she removed her clothes, opened her dresser, and under her sweaters pulled out her only means of satisfaction.

"You know," teased Donna one time after a really good fuck. "Their coal black skin would look so erotic meshed with your soft, white features."

"Oh my God!" Susan gasped in orgasm as she plunged the ten inch black vibrator into her horny, wet cunt.

At rest, Susan thought, "I'm gonna do it. I'll try and at least make Roger interested. I'll see what happens."

CHAPTER 3

Later that day, as Roger arrived home from school Susan was there to greet him. "Hi honey," Susan said with a nervous grin. "How was your day?'

"Uh, fine, mom." Roger couldn't help but notice Susan, all dolled up in her tight-fitting blouse and skirt. Roger hadn't seen her look this good in a long time. He didn't ask or say anything, but he did notice, and Susan could tell. As he left for his room, Susan thought "He noticed. He checked out my legs."

Once in his room, Roger laid down on his bed to rest. It didn't take long for the thought of his mom's shapely legs to enter his mind. "Why was she wearing that skirt?" he thought. Roger figured maybe she'd gone out or something. That evening was like any other: Dinner, homework, TV. With Ted tucked away in his study jacking off again, Susan figured she'd turn in early. She put a night shirt on that came only half-way down her thighs. Coming into the living room she turned to Roger lying on the couch and said "I'm going to bed sweetie. Goodnight."

Roger turned and once again caught sight of those shapely white legs. "Uh, okay." he replied. Susan turned and left the room, but not without bending down, pretending to pick something up. Roger caught sight of his mom's back thighs and panty-covered ass! "Fuck!" he thought. This was way unusual! Roger retired to his room a little while later, unable to concentrate on the TV. He felt weird. Uncomfortable. Roger was no virgin, and appreciated good-looking legs like any other guy, but his mom's? He thought about her and what was happening. She did have a nice body, after all. And real nice legs. He even remembered his friends, Greg and Paul, making lewd remarks about his mom in the past. They loved his mom's legs and that she was so hot. They even wanted to fuck her! It pissed Roger off, but now he could see why they desired her so. He'd just never paid attention. It made him think: those thighs, her calves. Ten minutes later, Roger was breathing heavily, furiously fisting his hard cock as he shot his load up into the air and down on his belly and fist.

The next morning Roger was almost frantic to get to school. This whole thing had him feeling more than a little guilty. When he got home, walking up the front walk he was nervous. What might happen? As luck would have it, upon entering the house his mom wasn't home. Roger breathed a sigh of relief. He went up to his room and saw an envelope addressed to him. As he opened it, he pulled out several pages. It looked like one of those erotic stories he often found while surfing the net. It was called "How I Got My Son To Fuck Me," by The Devil's Advocate.

"Hey, I like the The Devil's Advocate's stories," Roger thought, but then reality hit. Looking once again at the title "How I Got My Son..." Shit! Fuck! Nervously Roger read the story of a horny mom named Sabrina, who desired her son's cock after catching him masturbating and went for it by wearing less and less clothing around the house until she seduced him. Roger's cock was hard as a rock and he quickly jerked-off until he came yet again. When Roger finished and put his clothes back on he heard the front door open.

"Roger? Are you home?" Nervously Roger left his room and entered the kitchen where his mom was. "Hi honey, could you help me put these things away."

"Uh, sure, mom." Roger immediately noticed Susan's tight tee-shirt accentuating her breasts and her tight bike shorts showing off those legs again but also her shapely ass. God, she was hot. His friends weren't so sick after-all.

Later that evening, after dinner, Roger was once again up in his room reading the story.

"I guess she wants me," he thought. "Sex must be pretty bad with dad, if she's this desperate." Roger thought and thought. What were the pluses and minuses. Well, on the plus side, his mom was a really good-looking woman: great legs, tits, blond. "Yeah she IS nice. An older woman, that would be a first. I'll bet she can fuck like a real slut," he thought. Hey, this was his mom he was thinking about! "Oh, don't be such a fucking prude!" he scolded himself. "She wants it, you want it, go for it!"

Entering into the kitchen, Roger noticed his mom sitting at the table, on the phone with Donna. "He just turned nineteen," Donna said. "I measured him, too. Nine and three-quarters inches!"

Meanwhile, Roger headed straight for the refrigerator wearing only a pair of tight bike shorts that he seldom wore. He couldn't look his mother in the eye but she noticed his muscular chest, and strong legs. She tried not to look down towards his crotch, but as Roger nerved himself to look his moms way he caught her eyes checking out the bulge in his crotch. He smiled to himself. "This is fun," he thought. As Roger took his coke and walked away, his mom watched his tight butt as he left.

"Wouldn't you like to try it just once?" Donna asked.

"Um, hmm," Susan moaned watching her son disappear. After she got off the phone with Donna, Susan felt desperate. "Was he teasing me, too? What now? What's going on?" She felt so horny yet so unsure and insecure. She felt like it was time to talk to Roger. She wanted to but didn't know how to present her needs and feelings. It was obvious he noticed her and liked what he saw. She wanted him, too. "Oh, to hell with that, My god! It's incest, shit!' He's old enough. He knows what he's doing. Hell, he started it!" Susan thought.

Summoning the nerve, Susan headed toward Roger's room. "Where's Ted?" she thought. "Yeah, your husband. Remember?" Once again locked away in the study. "The bastard," she thought. Shaking like a little girl in the cold, Susan came within a foot of Roger's door. Preparing to knock she then heard something.

"Oh, yeah. Fuck." Roger moaned. Was he...jerking off? Closing her eyes, gritting her teeth, Susan thought "One, two, three," and opened his door. She let out a gasp as she saw her son's right hand fly up and down his erect cock.

"Mom!" Roger yelled and tried to cover himself up.

"Roger, I'm sorry, I really am." He sat up in bed, half-naked and mortified. Closing her eyes for a moment, Susan summoned the nerve.

"Listen honey," she said softly, closing the door behind her and moving closer to the bed. "I know. You have needs. I do, too..."

He stared at her in her robe as if expecting something to happen. Swallowing hard, Susan untied her robe and let it fall to the floor. Roger's eyes bugged out of his head.

"Let me," Susan said. "Let me do it. Please? I want to."

Susan then sat on the bed beside her handsome son. Brushing his hair off his forehead, she moved her hand down over his cheek and onto his chest. Down past his navel it went and then she pulled back his blanket. His cock was semi-hard and slick with his precum. Susan exhaled and swallowed hard. There was no turning back. Susan took her son's cock in hand and it quickly grew hard. Susan smiled and let out a nervous laugh. Roger also laughed. She began tugging at his cock until it was rock hard. All of a sudden Susan felt calm but very excited. Roger, too. They both wanted this.

"Oh, yeah, mom," Roger moaned. "Jerk it. Make me cum."

"Do you like that? Hmmm?"

"Yeah, mom."

"Oooohh. I wanna fuck my baby boy!"

"Suck it mom. Please?"

"You bet, stud."

Susan lowered her mouth down over the cockhead and took her son's cock into her mouth. She loved the taste of him. Sucking his cockhead she moaned around it, swirling her tongue, loving the taste.

"Oh fuck. What about dad?" Roger said in a panic.

"Don't worry about him. He's working as usual." With that she returned to sucking her son's cock. Susan went all the way down, deep-throating him, leaving a wet, warm trail of saliva dripping down to his balls.

"Ooohh, mom!" Roger moaned. "So good!"

Susan sucked and fisted the cock until Roger couldn't hold out any longer. He groaned and said he was going to cum. Susan's fist flew up and down, her mouth covering his cockhead as it blew its hot, sticky sperm into her mouth. Roger's body and cock jerked, his voice moaning and groaning as his sexy mom took his sperm down her throat. Susan swallowed every drop of her son's juice as if it was water for a parched throat.

"Oh wow mom! That was great."

"Thank you sweetie," she said and lowered her lips to his. "Listen, I better go before your father comes out from his cave." Getting up to grab her robe she turned back to her son and asked, "Do you like my body?"

"Fuck yeah, mom."

Susan quietly swayed in place, her hands going to her breasts, tweaking her nipples. Then working down to her cunt, which Roger had never seen before. She rubbed her wet pussy for him and then turned around giving her son a look at her ass. Swaying to an unheard rhythm, Susan accentuated her asscheeks with her hands and then in a show of sluttiness, spread her asscheeks giving her son a look at her puckered asshole. Big mistake! Roger's cock came roaring back to life. Noticing this, she muttered "Oh shit."

Roger's eyes looked so hungry but she really had better go.

"Listen," Susan said putting on her robe. "Tomorrow you can stay home from school. Okay?"

As she left, closing his door, she looked him in the eye, not as his mother but as his lover. He looked greedily back. They were both so excited. Neither of them got much sleep.

CHAPTER 4

When Susan woke the next morning she was excited but nervous as hell. She noticed her husband, Ted, lying there still not awake. How pathetic, she thought. A nice guy but a lousy lay. Even during the early years of their marriage Ted seemed more interested in watching porn flicks than actually fucking a real woman. It turned Susan off, but Ted's successful business allowed her to at least live the kind of life she'd always dreamed: nice house, family, she didn't have to work.

But that also left lots of time alone, and with a lousy sex life, lots of time to fantasize. The fantasies ran the gamut, from gangbangs to interracial. As she got older her fantasies changed somewhat. The men in her fantasies got younger and strangely, their cocks got bigger. Analyzing it, Susan figured that the younger men symbolized that she could still turn ...˜em on and the bigger cocks, well...after years with Ted she would liked to have tried something new. Her friend Donna's young, black stud conquests didn't help.

After many years of marriage Susan had a quickie affair with Ted's old business partner but that ended when he and his family moved out of state. A few years later came what

Susan referred to in her mind as "the accidental affair." It was great but she didn't want to think about it. It happened a few times, ended badly, and that was that. Now, a year later, she was about to have the first passionate sex since then: with her teenage son.

Susan got up, put on her robe and headed for the kitchen to start a pot of coffee. Ted came in a few minutes later, dressed and ready for work. Then Roger walked in, quietly, nervously. Mother and son looked at each other. With Ted looking at the front page of the paper, they made eye contact.

Susan winked and Roger smiled. Roger would pretend to go to school and just walk back to the house after dad was gone, since they both left around the same time every morning. When father and son were heading out the door Susan said "Have a nice day." Roger could only laugh. As Ted got in his car, Roger started walking down the street, slowly, deliberately. Then Ted drove by him waving. Roger waved back. Pretending to stop and tie his shoe, Roger waited for Ted's car to completely disappear down the road, turned around and headed back to the house.

"I wonder what's going on?" Ted thought. "I wonder if anything's happening with them? I better come up with some plan to see if MY plans are moving forward."

Meanwhile, Roger walked in the front door and quickly locked it.

"Mom?" he called out.

"In here," Susan called from Roger's room.

Roger walked hurriedly into his room, threw down his book bag and looked towards the bed. There was his mom under the covers. Just then she pulled them down revealing her breasts and pussy. Roger's eyes bulged along with something else. Lifting her legs, Susan parted them to show her son her wet pussy. She began playing with it, rubbing her clit, and plunging her fingers in and out of her hot, sweaty cunt.

"Come and get it," she beckoned huskily. Roger quickly got out of his clothes and frantically tried to get his pants off, his mom laughing at his attempts. Finally! There he stood. The teen Adonis with his cock high and hard.

"Oh baby," Susan moaned. "Give momma some dick!"

As Roger made his way to Susan's head, she reached out and took hold of his cock. She caressed it, rubbing his oozing precum all around the now glistening shaft.

"Mom, suck it. Please!" She did, taking the cock into her mouth. Susan sucked her son's cock like a whore in heat, moaning around it, slobbering all over it, dripping saliva onto the sheets. Roger moaned and groaned unable to take much more of this. Susan stopped, took the cock out of her mouth and said, "Here honey, lie down. Let me get on top of you."

"Can I fuck your ass, mom?"

"You better," she replied with a giggle. "We're gonna do everything!"

"Maybe I don't have to go to school ever again!"

"Ha, ha, don't count on it! But maybe I'll talk your father into letting you stay home from the store on Saturday. That way while he's taking care of business, you can take care of mine! How's that sound?"

"Great mom."

"Mmmm, I'm so glad you left me that story," Susan said, snuggling with her son.

"What story?" Roger asked.

"What do you mean 'what story'? The one in your hamper."

"What are you talking about?" Roger asked.

"The story in your hamper a few days ago. I was doing your laundry and found it. Remember?"

"Mom, I don't know what you're talking about. What kind of story?"

Susan lay silent for a moment in confusion. "About the mother and son," she replied.

"You mean the one you sent me?" Roger asked.

Confused, Susan asked "What did I send you?"

"That story about ..."

"About what?" Susan asked.

"About a mother and son..." Roger said his voice trailing off.

"I didn't send you anything." she replied, getting up in the bed to confront her son.

"Well I didn't leave you any incest story," Roger countered.

"Yeah, well I didn't mail you one!" she fired back.

They both were silent. Finally Roger asked, "Well who did?"

Susan was quiet for a moment. Piercing her eyes in another direction, she grew angry.

"Mom, what is it?"

Letting out an exasperated sigh, Susan said "Honey, I think we've been set up!"

"Set up?"

"Um, hmm. The person who mailed you that "story" was the one who left ME one, too!" Then looking into her son's eyes she said, "And only one other person had access to your hamper."

"DAD!?"

"Yep! It had to be your father."

"But why?"

After a pause, Susan replied "I don't know exactly." Then another pause. "I guess it was some sick fantasy of his."

"Why?" Roger asked.

Angrily, she replied "To see us DOING it! A mother and son, I mean."

"But he's not even here!" Roger said.

"I know," Susan replied. "But maybe he hopes one day - Oh, I don't know! Your father's strange when it comes to certain things." Roger looked at her trying to comprehend the situation. Realizing he needed further explaining, Susan said "Your dad - some men - they have fantasies...I don't know. It's hard to explain."

"You mean about incest?" he asked.

"Well, that... and about older women...their MOTHERS!"

After a few moments Roger spoke up. "Obviously Dad wanted us... to do this."

"Obviously," Susan replied, a little hurt

"Does he want to watch us, do you think?"

"Probably," she replied remembering the porn video days.

"Like he's setting us up where he knows we're doing it and then can watch us at some point?"

Susan smiled at her son. "You're very wise," she said. "I think that's what he has planned."

"Well, what do you want to do about it?" Roger asked.

"Let me think about it," she said. "In the meantime," she said grabbing her son's flaccid cock. "Maybe we can get this hard. You want to fuck my ass, right? Your father started this, so let's finish it! Come on," she said stroking her son's cock back to life. "Fuck mommy's ass!"

Roger did that and more for the next several hours. By the time Ted got home, his wife was one well-fucked whore. And Roger hadn't had so much sex in his life.

Later that evening, before going to bed, Susan came into Roger's room to kiss him goodnight. "How about if we give your father a show?"

Roger was shocked. "Right now?" he asked.

"No, but soon."

"You want to do it in front of him?" Roger asked, rather uncertain.

"Oh, hell, no. I have a better idea. He's not getting away with his sick fantasies at our expense. I want to set HIM up! You want to have some fun with your perverted father?"

"You mean get even?" Roger replied.

"Uh, huh?" Susan said with a wicked little smile.

"Yeah," Roger replied. "If he can fuck with us, let's fuck with HIM, too!"

CHAPTER 5

Saturdays had become the best days for Susan and Roger to get together. Roger could only take just so much time off from school and on Sundays, Ted closed his business. Roger often worked on Saturdays with Ted to earn a little extra money, but Susan was now encouraging Roger to stay home.

"Don't worry," she told him. "I'll give you a little extra every week, as long you give ME a little extra!" Roger agreed and asked his father if he always needed to come in on Saturdays. Normally Ted would have been annoyed because he'd have to hire a part-time employee for those half-days but he quickly figured it out.

"Maybe it's starting to happen," he wondered. He'd already noticed the changes in his wife. She was wearing less around the house. Shorts that got shorter; skirts that now came up several inches above her knee. She was getting her hair done regularly, putting on more make-up and perfume. She and Roger tried to act like nothing was going on but since Ted was looking for it, he noticed the changes. He also noticed how hot his wife looked and wanted to finally fuck her again, himself; not that he had any plans on doing that! No, no, this was his ultimate fantasy, to see his wife and son in the throes of full-blown fucking passion and he started to feel that, well, maybe it was working.

So he granted Roger's request and then started to feel "Hey, business is okay. Maybe I don't have to open shop on Saturdays anymore!" What a great excuse. Pretend to go to work and then drive home an hour later. The thought excited Ted so much it made him hard.

The first few weeks together, Susan and Roger tried everything: sixty-nine, anal; fucking in his bed, her bed, the living room couch, the shower. Susan even wanted to fuck on her husband's desk in the study but was afraid they'd mess everything up. Instead, when they fucked in her bed, she always made sure they fucked on Ted's side of the bed. It was the ultimate betrayal but the fucking bastard deserved it!

Susan was quickly becoming a changed woman. She was horny as hell, all the time now. All the years of lousy sex had made the forty year-old blond a spouting geyser, a faucet that just wouldn't shut itself off. Even when Donna called to inform her of how many black studs she screwed yesterday, Susan could only smirk. "If she only knew who I fucked yesterday!" Yes, life was good!

Then came the moment of truth. Ted sensed something was indeed going on, and it excited him like crazy, bringing back memories of his friend, James, royally fucking his mom, Sandy, all those years ago. (With no knowledge that his slut, whore-mom was doing ALL his friends!)

On this particular Saturday, Ted woke, showered, dressed and made a quick breakfast for himself, not wishing to disturb his still-sleeping wife. He left the house around nine, driving to work with a raging hard-on. By the time he got to the shop, Ted paced around nervously, waiting for the clock to strike ten. Then even more nervously, he closed, and headed for the parking lot and his car. Twenty minutes later he was home, sweating bullets. What might be going on, he wondered.

As Ted parked the car on the street, he slowly made his way up the walk until he reached the door. "What if nothing's gong on?" he thought. "How do I explain myself?" Ted figured he'd make some excuse, and slowly let himself inside his own house, like a thief in the night. When he entered all was silent. He walked into the living room but no sign of his wife or son. As Ted quietly made his way further inside the house he thought he heard something. Noises - coming from Roger's room! Catching his breath, Ted tip-toed down the hall until he got within a few feet of Roger's room. Then he heard it all.

"Oh, yes! Oh god, Roger! Yeah, that's it! Oh! Oh! Oh! Yes! Yes! Yes! Oh god, fuck me!

Harder! Harder! Fuck your momma's pussy! Harder!! Oooohhh, gooooodd!"

Ted stopped in his tracks! Nervously peeking around the doorway to his son's room he saw an amazing sight. There, on his son's bed was his wife, on all fours, with her son behind her, pounding his cock, hard and fast, in and out of his mother's cunt.

"Ah yeah!" Roger cried. "Oh, I'm gonna cum mom! I'm gonna cum!"

"Yes baby!" Susan cried. "Cum in me! Give mommy your cum!"

Roger thrust wildly now, his face contorted, sweat glistening on his young frame, as he furiously pounded his teenaged cock in and out of his mom's cunt. Susan was in ecstasy. Her eyes glazed, her mouth ajar, panting, gasping with each thrust her son's thick, hard prick in and out of her whorish cunt.

Ted was in a state of shock. Here at last was his ultimate fantasy. His own wife was fucking their teenaged son! Watching the scene unfold just ten feet away from him caused Ted's little dick to become rock hard.

"Oh yeah!" Roger cried. Here it comes! Aaahhh!" Then his prick began twitching, shooting his hot, sticky sperm inside his mom's cunt.

"Ooohhhh!!" Susan moaned. "Give it to me!" she cried, feeling her own boy's juices go shooting inside of her. "Give me your cum! Give mommy your cum!"

Susan collapsed on her son's bed as Roger pulled his slick cock from her cunt. Ted then backed away from the door in fear. Lying down beside her, mother and son cuddled for a few minutes, cooing in the afterglow of a truly damn good fuck. Just then, Susan spoke up. "Hello Honey! We know you're out there!"

A stunned Ted was left speechless in the hall.

"Ted, get your ass in here!!!" his wife screamed.

As Ted nervously entered she set him straight.

"We know what you did?" she said calmly. "Why you did it, I don't want to know. But now that you've gotten your wish to see a mother and son fuck, here's some news for you. We LIKE it! Did you hear me? I LOVE fucking my son! YOUR son! It's better than any sex I ever had with YOU! You and your pathetic little dick! Kissing Roger on the cheek Susan cooed "And do you like fucking mommy?"

"Yeah!" Roger exclaimed, looking his father in the eye. "I LOVE it!"

"Good. From now on YOU'RE my man! When I need to get fucked, I'm gonna fuck ONLY my SON!" Then adding a mean, shit-eating grin, Susan looked at Ted and said

"NOT his father." Susan laughed to herself and staring at Ted thought "Gotcha! You bastard!"

CHAPTER 6

As the weeks progressed, Susan and Roger continued their incestuous ways.

But now with Ted out in the open about setting them up for his own selfish desires, it took on a new twist. For openers Roger could go back to work on Saturdays because he and his mom were fucking every night. Every evening, at Susan's insistence, they would all retire to the master bedroom and get naked. Susan would get into bed with her son and the fireworks would begin. Roger was loving it. He felt his father deserved it and yet was almost appreciative of his perversions. After all, if it wasn't for his sick old man, he'd never have gotten this chance to fuck his hot mom!

And mom was getting hotter and sluttier by the week! Susan would have Roger lie down on the bed with his raging erection. "Get in the chair," she would instruct her husband. Ted's punishment for his set-up was he could watch but not take part. He could only jerk off to the sight of his wife fucking their son but would have no further claim to her. Her body now belonged to Roger, and Ted had no choice but to accept it. His reward was he could watch and jerk off but nothing else.

Once she had Roger lie down on the bed, Susan would straddle his face so he could eat her pussy. Then facing her husband she'd lower herself down to take her son's cock into her mouth. Ted would be forced to watch as his wife sucked off their son, all the while staring intently into his eyes as she slobbered all over Roger's cock. Susan was loving every minute of what was going on and what she was becoming. A controlling, fucking slut!

"Do it!" she screamed at Ted one time, as he just stared at her cocksucking. Susan pulled her mouth off of Roger's cock and snapped at her staring husband. "Jerk off, damn it! If you don't start playing with yourself this all comes to an end right now!" Ted would go back to stroking himself while his wife took their son's cock back into her mouth, all the while never taking her eyes off of her husband's. "I really married a cuckold," she thought. "He likes to watch me with other men." Susan was coming up with some new ideas, some really big plans for Ted. And herself.

After Roger would cum down his mom's throat, Susan would get off of him and ask him which hole he wanted to fuck tonight. On this particular night Roger wanted it good and tight. As Susan got on all fours, Roger lubed himself up and got behind his mother.

"Oh yeah, baby!" Susan cried. "Fuck my ass! Work that cock of yours up my asshole!" Roger started inching his way up his mom's anus, loving her hot tight hole. Meanwhile Susan, as always, facing Ted, would look him in the eye and put on a show.

"Oh god, Ted! He's fucking me! Your son is fucking me up the ASS! Oh, his cock is soooo goooood! So much BIGGER than yours! So much better than you ever were! Oh yes, Roger! Yeah, that's good! Fuck mommy's ass! Shoot your cum up my AAASSS!"

Roger started thrusting wildly, pounding his cock up his mom's ass as far as he could go, breathing heavily, groaning loudly.

"Yeah baby!" Susan cried. "Cum! Cum! Cum for me! Cum in my ass! Shoot in me Roger!"

Meanwhile, Ted was sitting on the chair, frantically pulling on his cock, watching his wife get nailed in the rear by his own son.

"Oh! Ahhh! Yeah! I'm cumming! Cumming!" Roger cried as he shot his load deep up his mom's bowels.

"Oh yeah, honey," Susan moaned. "Mmmm, I feel it!"

"Aaahh! Yeah!" Roger screamed unleashing more and more sperm.

"Ooohhh!" Susan cried, as she took more of her son's sperm up her ass.

"Aaahh!" Ted cried, as he shot his semen onto the floor.

When it was all over, and Roger had gone back to his room for the night, Ted laid in bed as Susan stepped out of her nightly bath; sore but satisfied.

"Did you enjoy that?" she asked in a condescending tone. "You shot a big load onto the floor earlier. I'm really beginning to think you like seeing a cock up my ass more than my cunt."

Ted was enjoying it but after several weeks, night after night, he was getting a wee bit bored. Maybe the fantasy had run its course.

"How much longer are we gonna do this?" he asked.

"What? Me fucking Roger in front of you?" Susan asked with arms folded. "I'm surprised, Ted. I thought you wanted this. We're only giving you what you want."

Lying down in bed Susan asked "What else do you want us to do Teddy? We've done everything in front of you." Then pausing for a moment she reminded him, "You're not taking part, you know."

Ted was annoyed by that. He may have been a voyeur but he still wanted to fuck his wife at least once before he died. Since this whole thing had begun Susan, in anger, and enjoying being in control, wouldn't even let Ted touch her. Then Susan had a wicked thought. "Maybe you'd like to see others. Hmm? Is that what you want, dear? Do you want to see me with other men? Like so many other husbands do? Or maybe just young men. That's really what you want now isn't it? To watch me fuck a group of teenage studs? Would that appeal to your mommy fantasies? Mom does the neighborhood, Mom does the school, the football team -"

"Alright!" Ted snapped. "Enough." Ted just stared straight ahead, not letting on that he was excited.

"Should I have Roger bring over his friends?" Susan asked. "I'm serious, Ted. They can ALL fuck me! Would you like to watch me take on Roger's friends? I could go for some bigger cocks."

What? Ted was stunned. "What do you mean?" he managed to say. Susan was flustered. "Oh, well, what I mean is, well it's just that, Roger is, you know, kind of like you. I mean he's bigger than you, but that's not saying very much."

"Is that what you want?" Ted asked with a feeling of great anxiety. "You want to fuck other men?" For the first time in weeks, Susan started to feel nervous and out of control.

"I don't want that," Ted said firmly. "Look. I fucked up, alright? I had a fantasy that I just should have kept to myself instead of dragging you guys into it." Susan laid there in bed, staring straight ahead, angry and hurt.

"You want another cock, fine, he's down the hall," Ted said. "Let's just keep this to ourselves. It seems to me you're getting what you want. Roger, too." Turning to confront her husband, Susan said "You have no idea of what I want. What I need. You never have." With that Susan turned out the light and they both lay angry in the darkness.

The next night, Susan called Roger to her bedroom. He undressed as she went looking for Ted. She found him in his study.

"We're waiting for you," she said.

"Enjoy yourselves," he said without looking up. Susan was stunned. "I, I thought you wanted this?"

"Susan, forget it," he said. "Just forget it. You don't need me there to fuck Roger."

"The only reason I'm fucking Roger is for you," she said firmly. "He's my son and I love him and I want to help him get his needs met, but trust me, in the cock department he isn't my first choice." Ted was angered by that but never looked up. "Fine," Susan said and stormed off.

Walking into her room, Roger was surprised. "Where's dad?" he asked.

"Oh, well, he can't be bothered tonight, so it's just us."

"He doesn't want to do this anymore?" Roger asked. Susan was about to speak but Roger interrupted. "Good," he said. "I'm getting tired of his perverted stuff." Susan was stunned.

"Wha, what do you mean?" she asked.

"Don't get me wrong, mom. I'm glad we're doing it but I'm tired of doing it in front of him. Let's just you and I do it."

"Oh," Susan said meekly. Roger just laid back stroking his hard cock as Susan quietly got on the bed, knelt down and took it in her mouth. After a few licks and kisses on Roger's cock, Susan took it out of her mouth and asked "So I guess you're not into anymore fun and games, either, huh?"

"What do you mean?" he asked.

"Well, I thought that maybe we could do something a bit wilder for your father. That maybe it's getting boring. Especially since your dad likes to see another guy's cock in me."

"What do you mean? I thought he just wanted to see us doing it?"

"Yes Roger, he does, but he's also one of those husbands that likes to see his wife with other men. It's partly that, partly his son fucking his own mother, partly the younger man-older woman thing. It's all intertwined."

After saying that, Roger looked confused. Taking his cock back into her mouth, Susan thought deeply about the next thing on her mind. Removing his cock from her mouth Susan looked up at her son and asked "How would you feel if we expanded our games somewhat?"

"What do you mean, mom?"

"I mean, like if we invited someone else to take part -"

"What!?" Roger snapped. Susan developed a knot in the pit of her stomach.

"What do you mean, mom? Like who? You want to fuck someone else?"

"No sweetheart, it's just that your dad likes this and -

"Fuck dad!" Then after a nervous pause, Roger, his curiosity equaled only by his anxiety managed to ask, "Who mom? Like what did you have in mind?"

"Well, I just thought that maybe we could have some fun and jazz things up a bit if you, well, might like to invite some friends over -"

"My friends?" Roger snapped. "You want to fuck my friends?!"

"No! It's for your father!"

"Bullshit mom!"

"Roger, I am not! Why would I mention this if I wasn't thinking about your father and you and -"

"Forget it!" Roger snapped. With that he quickly got off his parents bed and ran off to his room, slamming the door behind him.

"Oh fuck," Susan thought. She was in deep shit now.

CHAPTER 7

On a Wednesday, a couple of weeks later, Ted turned off the computer in his office and made his way out front where his staff was dealing with their jobs and customers. Turning to Jane, his assistant manager Ted said "I think I'm going to go home for lunch, Jane."

"Okay, Ted. See you later." Ted got in his car and drove home which was only about fifteen minutes away. Pulling up the street he noticed Susan's car in the driveway. "Damn," he thought. Things were so bad at home they were hardly talking to each other. Ted knew he had to find some way of patching things up. For the first time in years he was truly afraid they might be heading towards divorce. Maybe this was a good time to talk about it.

As Ted entered the front door, the house was eerily silent. Then he thought he heard noises coming from his bedroom. They were very familiar. Annoyed Ted thought "Oh fuck, not again. That kid has missed more school lately." Ted was annoyed that his wife was turning into such a slut, fucking Roger whenever she felt like it, and his grades would soon be a concern if this kept up.

As Ted got closer to his room, he was filled with conflict. He didn't want to look, he wanted to end this nightmare, but he was weak. He really did love to see his wife fucking their son. He really enjoyed watching her with a teenage cock plowing her hot holes, or her sucking him off. Oh what the hell. As he crept quietly toward the door not wanting them to know he was home, and watching again, he heard Susan more plainly now. Her moans were deep, guttural. When she said things like "Oh god, yeah! Fuck me harder! Deeper!" it was different. Wow, Roger was getting good!

"Ooooohh! Ooooohhh! Yeah, fuck my ass harder! Harder! Harder! Oooohhh, I love it!"

"Fucking whore," Ted thought he heard Roger reply.

"Yeah, I am a whore! I'm YOUR whore! Oh, god, I love it!"

As Susan wailed and screamed and cried in delight, Ted took a peek around the corner. His eyes bulged and mouth fell. There was Susan on the bed on her hands and knees, taking a cock deep up her ass, while another cock was beneath her, thrusting in and out of her cunt! The guys faces were obstructed from Ted but their sweaty bodies moved together in unison fucking his wife.

"Oooohhh, fuck my ass! Fuck my cunt! Oh, I'm gonna cum again!"

"God, I love this whore's asshole!" came the male voice fucking her ass. "How's her pussy, man?"

"Great as usual! Ahh, shit yeah! Gonna cum!"

"Yeeess! Cum in me! Fill me with your cum!"

Ted was shocked. "Great as usual?" He was stunned, totally floored by the sight of his wife getting fucked by two guys, and obviously not for the first time.

"Oh god, Greg!" Susan cried. "Fuck me faster! Harder! Harder!!"

Greg? Oh my god, Ted thought. Greg! And Paul was fucking Susan's ass!

Greg and Paul. Roger's friends!

"Yeah! Yeah! Ahh, cumming!" Paul cried as he thrust his cock wildly in and out of Susan's asshole. Meanwhile, Greg thrust his prick up her hot, wet and cumming pussy. Ted watched the three sweaty bodies fuck like they were meant for each other. Susan let out one continuous cry of orgasmic pleasure and then collapsed on top of Greg. He held her, thrusting his prick up inside her cunt, while Paul held her hips tightly to his, as he stood there breathing hard, unloading his seed deep up Susan's bowels.

"Ah, yeah! Yeah! Yeah!" Greg groaned as he just held Susan, his own cock twitching and cumming deep inside her cunt. When Paul pulled his prick out of Susan's ass, Ted was floored again. Wow! Visions of his old buddy James came to mind. A young man with a very manly prick! Long and thick and soiled with his own cum foaming around it. Ted noticed Susan's asshole, stretched wide open from the anal assault, with lots of cum oozing out. Ted couldn't believe how much cum Paul had shot into her, but his assumption was wrong. Both guys had been fucking her since mid-morning and both had unloaded a gallon of cum not only deep up Susan's ass, but her cunt, too, as well as down her throat.

Then Susan rolled off of Greg and he, too, sported a sticky-wet, huge cock that was finally deflating. Greg and Paul made even Roger look small. Ted backed away from the door and listened from out in the hall.

"God, you guys are so fucking good," Susan moaned.

"You are, too," said one voice. Ted heard sounds coming from the bathroom.

"What time is it?" she asked.

"Twelve forty-five. Man I'm hungry!"

"I'm tired!" Susan replied and then laughed. "I'm so sore. I need a bath."

"We're worth it, aren't we?" came the other voice.

"Always!" she replied.

Ted realized he'd better leave right there, and did. He backed away, and quietly made his way out the front door, quickly got in his car and drove off. He was stunned, silent, feeling defeated. My god, how little he knew about things, especially his own wife. Susan was a total slut in there. She was fucking Roger's friends and apparently she'd done this before!

"I wonder if Roger knows? Nah, no way. He'd probably kill her. Either that or break down."

Ted couldn't believe that his own wife would do that. Coercing her into fucking their son was one thing, but this was of her own making. Ted couldn't get the thought out of his mind. Watching his forty year-old wife being double penetrated by those two huge teenage cocks. She was fucking Roger's friends and was loving it! His own wife: a slut, a whore, a size queen. Ted then noticed his own cock was rock hard and leaking in his pants.

CHAPTER 8

On a Wednesday, a couple of weeks later, Ted turned off the computer in his office and made his way out front where his staff was dealing with their jobs and customers. Turning to Jane, his assistant manager Ted said "I think I'm going to go home for lunch, Jane."

"Okay, Ted. See you later." Ted got in his car and drove home which was only about fifteen minutes away. Pulling up the street he noticed Susan's car in the driveway. "Damn," he thought. Things were so bad at home they were hardly talking to each other. Ted knew he had to find some way of patching things up. For the first time in years he was truly afraid they might be heading towards divorce. Maybe this was a good time to talk about it.

As Ted entered the front door, the house was eerily silent. Then he thought he heard noises coming from his bedroom. They were very familiar. Annoyed Ted thought "Oh fuck, not again. That kid has missed more school lately." Ted was annoyed that his wife was turning into such a slut, fucking Roger whenever she felt like it, and his grades would soon be a concern if this kept up.

As Ted got closer to his room, he was filled with conflict. He didn't want to look, he wanted to end this nightmare, but he was weak. He really did love to see his wife fucking their son. He really enjoyed watching her with a teenage cock plowing her hot holes, or her sucking him off. Oh what the hell. As he crept quietly toward the door not wanting them to know he was home, and watching again, he heard Susan more plainly now. Her moans were deep, guttural. When she said things like "Oh god, yeah! Fuck me harder! Deeper!" it was different. Wow, Roger was getting good!

"Ooooohh! Ooooohhh! Yeah, fuck my ass harder! Harder! Harder! Ooooohhh, I love it!"

"Fucking whore," Ted thought he heard Roger reply.

"Yeah, I am a whore! I'm YOUR whore! Oh, god, I love it!"

As Susan wailed and screamed and cried in delight, Ted took a peek around the corner. His eyes bulged and mouth fell. There was Susan on the bed on her hands and knees, taking a cock deep up her ass, while another cock was beneath her, thrusting in and out of her cunt! The guys faces were obstructed from Ted but their sweaty bodies moved together in unison fucking his wife.

"Oooohhh, fuck my ass! Fuck my cunt! Oh, I'm gonna cum again!"

"God, I love this whore's asshole!" came the male voice fucking her ass. "How's her pussy, man?"

"Great as usual! Ahh, shit yeah! Gonna cum!"

"Yeeess! Cum in me! Fill me with your cum!"

Ted was shocked. "Great as usual?" He was stunned, totally floored by the sight of his wife getting fucked by two guys, and obviously not for the first time.

"Oh god, Greg!" Susan cried. "Fuck me faster! Harder! Harder!!"

Greg? Oh my god, Ted thought. Greg! And Paul was fucking Susan's ass!

Greg and Paul. Roger's friends!

"Yeah! Yeah! Ahh, cumming!" Paul cried as he thrust his cock wildly in and out of Susan's asshole. Meanwhile, Greg thrust his prick up her hot, wet and cumming pussy. Ted watched the three sweaty bodies fuck like they were meant for each other. Susan let out one continuous cry of orgasmic pleasure and then collapsed on top of Greg. He held her, thrusting his prick up inside her cunt, while Paul held her hips tightly to his, as he stood there breathing hard, unloading his seed deep up Susan's bowels.

"Ah, yeah! Yeah! Yeah!" Greg groaned as he just held Susan, his own cock twitching and cumming deep inside her cunt. When Paul pulled his prick out of Susan's ass, Ted was floored again. Wow! Visions of his old buddy James came to mind. A young man with a very manly prick! Long and thick and soiled with his own cum foaming around it. Ted noticed Susan's asshole, stretched wide open from the anal assault, with lots of cum oozing out. Ted couldn't believe how much cum Paul had shot into her, but his assumption was wrong. Both guys had been fucking her since mid-morning and both had unloaded a gallon of cum not only deep up Susan's ass, but her cunt, too, as well as down her throat.

Then Susan rolled off of Greg and he, too, sported a sticky-wet, huge cock that was finally deflating. Greg and Paul made even Roger look small. Ted backed away from the door and listened from out in the hall.

"God, you guys are so fucking good," Susan moaned.

"You are, too," said one voice. Ted heard sounds coming from the bathroom.

"What time is it?" she asked.

"Twelve forty-five. Man I'm hungry!"

"I'm tired!" Susan replied and then laughed. "I'm so sore. I need a bath."

"We're worth it, aren't we?" came the other voice.

"Always!" she replied.

Ted realized he'd better leave right there, and did. He backed away, and quietly made his way out the front door, quickly got in his car and drove off. He was stunned, silent, feeling defeated. My god, how little he knew about things, especially his own wife. Susan was a total slut in there. She was fucking Roger's friends and apparently she'd done this before!

"I wonder if Roger knows? Nah, no way. He'd probably kill her. Either that or break down."

Ted couldn't believe that his own wife would do that. Coercing her into fucking their son was one thing, but this was of her own making. Ted couldn't get the thought out of his mind. Watching his forty year-old wife being double penetrated by those two huge teenage cocks. She was fucking Roger's friends and was loving it! His own wife: a slut, a whore, a size queen. Ted then noticed his own cock was rock hard and leaking in his pants.

CHAPTER 9

"We're all set," Susan informed her husband who was lying in bed waiting for her. "That was fast," Ted replied.

"I know," Susan said. "Thank goodness for e-mail. You know what Greg's e-mail address is? 8nhard." Susan laughed but Ted was just a little concerned. Taking off her clothes and getting in bed, Ted asked Susan "Are you sure you wanna go through with this?"

"Of course," she replied. "Don't tell me you're getting cold feet!"

"No, no, it's just that I don't want you doing anything that -"

"Ted, I want to. Trust me. You saw for yourself. When I'm with Greg and Paul I become a real slut. Having them invite other boys is fine with me. I've never been gangbanged before. I'm REALLY looking forward to it." Stopping to think, Susan said, "You know, one of these days I ought to write all this down as a story and you can submit it to your sex-story site. What is it, Lito -"

"Literotica," Ted answered.

"Yeah. Maybe it'll turn on a lot of people," Susan said "But for now, it's time for your reward." Susan leaned over and pulled Ted's cock out of his pajama bottoms.

"Nice and hard for me, I see. I know what you're thinking about, you nasty boy," she said licking and sucking and kissing Ted's cock. "You're so hard over what mommy's gonna do this weekend in that motel room with all your classmates. Mommy's gonna suck their cocks and let them fuck mommy in her cunt, and then they're gonna take their huge cocks and shove them deep up mommy's ass! Does my little weeny-boy wanna see that, hmm?" Ted groaned and then shot his load down mommy's, er, his wife's throat.

That Saturday, Susan and Ted had it all arranged. Ted made an excuse to Roger that he needed his help at work and Susan convinced Roger to go promising that next Saturday would be super-special. Susan didn't want to be too sore after Roger fucked her. She wanted to be one hundred percent whole and horny for that evening. About seven that night, Ted and Susan dressed and when they came out Roger looked surprised.

"Where are you going?" he asked.

"Oh, we're going out to dinner, sweetie," his mom replied.

"Yeah, uh, we'll be back in a few hours," Ted mumbled.

"A few hours?" Roger asked almost laughing. "That's not dinner, that's a feast!"

"Yeah, I'm gonna feast on your friends' big cocks," Susan thought. As they walked out, Roger thought he'd call his friends to maybe get together or something.

"Uh, no man, I can't," Greg replied, lying over the phone. "I've got family here, you know, and I can't tonight. As a matter of fact, we're going out in a bit so -"

Over the phone Paul lied too, but with more mischief. "Sorry Dave. Gotta date tonight."

"You?" Roger asked. "Since when?'

"Well, since I met this older woman. A friend of my mom's you could say." Roger was shocked. "Are you fucking her?"

"Yeah, man, she's a fucking whore for it!" Paul replied. "She likes young guys, man."

"Maybe you can introduce me to her!" Roger said with excitement.

"Uh, yeah, I guess. Maybe one day. Look I gotta go now, okay?"

"Have fun," Roger said.

"With YOUR mom it ALWAYS is," Paul thought hanging up.

By the time Susan and Ted reached the motel he was quiet and nervous. Susan, too, was nervous but excited. After paying for a room, Ted and Susan entered. While Ted watched for Roger's friends, Susan went into the bathroom to change into the outfit the guys wanted her to wear. Even Ted had no idea what she would wear. It was one of many surprises that they all had for each other that evening. About ten minutes later two cars pulled up. When the occupants stepped out, Ted quickly motioned for them to enter the room. He was all but speechless; a nervous, excited wreck as Greg, Paul and three other young men made their way inside the motel room.

"Got any beer?" one guys asked sitting on the bed.

"Uh, no, I uh -"

"Maybe later," Greg interjected.

"So. Where's our whore-slut?" Paul asked.

"You really don't mind this?" another guy asked Ted. He didn't answer, instead knocking on the bathroom door to let Susan know they'd arrived. "Man, I'd never let my wife fuck around, let alone want to watch!" the guy said.

"Then you better not be home tomorrow afternoon," joked Greg. "We'll all be fucking YOUR mom in your own bed!" The guys broke up with laughter, and then Susan stepped into the room.

"Fuck!" said one guy. "Yeah," Greg chimed in, and there was a whistle or two. For the young studs their whore had arrived. Susan wore a super-tight tee shirt, faded tiny cut-offs accentuating her fine creamy-white legs, cut all the way up to her asscheeks, and a pair of red pumps that made her sexy calves even more so. Her ruby-red lipstick and blond hair coming down to her shoulders gave a look that said "Come fuck me, boys!" As Susan looked over the crowd she was stunned. She didn't even know these three other guys.

"This is Steve, Pete, and Jerry," Greg said.

"Uh, hi," Susan managed to say, staring into their eager yet handsome faces. "And this is Roger's mom. Our slut," Greg told them. "She loves huge young cocks and she's gonna get plenty of it!"

Susan was expecting different guys and as Greg came up to give her a wet kiss, she whispered, "Who are these guys?" Where are -"

"Oh, I chose these three for a reason," he said. "Relax." With that he kissed her and plunged his tongue into her mouth. Then Paul got up to kiss her, too. Then Greg said "Why doesn't our whore greet the new guys with a proper kiss!" A little unsure, Susan looked at Ted, but Greg nudged her and she made her way to Steve and kissed him, tentatively but he grabbed her and thrust his tongue inside. Susan then walked over to Pete and kissed him, too. Finally she smiled nervously at Jerry and kissed him, as well. All the while, Ted just sat in the chair stunned to see his wife kissing with these young guys, three of them total strangers!

Then Greg pulled out a mini boom box and turned a tape on. It was a sexy dance number. "Why don't you strip for us? Put on a real good show, too!" Susan looked at Ted who just sat there like a little kid, saying nothing, but certainly not about to stop anything, either. Susan took in a deep breath and began to dance around to the beat, swaying her hips, using her hands to accentuate her body. Noticing how eager her audience was boosted Susan's confidence. She then reached for her shirt and seductively pulled it off revealing her fine-looking breasts, and, by now very erect nipples. Then Susan undid the button on her cut-offs, and slowly brought the zipper down, letting the shorts fall to the floor.

"Damn," one guy said. "Fucking great ass," another chimed in. "Why don't you show the boys that fucking great ass, slut!" Greg said. Susan knew just what he was referring, too. Something that all sluts do for their studs. Stepping out of the cut-offs, Susan turned

going in and out, to and fro, over and over, harder and faster, frantically fucking her, Susan let the cock in her mouth slip out and she screamed in pleasure. "Ooooohhhh! Ooooohhh! Oh, I'm gonna cum! Oh yeah! Oh yeah! Ooooooohhhh, cumming!

Gasping and squealing, Susan's juices began to overflow in orgasmic ecstasy. Meanwhile the boys could hold out no longer. The guy who Susan had been blowing, started jerking off and along with Greg and Paul, all three groaned in pleasure shooting their cum all over her face, her back and onto her tits. Then the cock thrusting up and down in her cunt began to twitch as its owner cried out "Oh yeah! Oh yeah! Ahh!" and came in her cunt. Then the guy behind her held Susan's limp body and banged her ass for all he was worth finally screaming "Yeah! Yeah! Ahh, cumming! Fuck!" and he unloaded deep in her bowels.

Meanwhile, Ted was still fisting his cock, in awe of everything he'd seen. Yet to cum, he watched Greg, Paul and the other guy back away, all three fatigued. Then the guy who fucked his wife's ass backed away and the cock in her pussy plopped out. Ted noticed his wife's used ass, the hole gaping open, leaking sperm into the sperm oozing from her cunt. "Ahh!" Ted cried, cumming at the sight of Susan's wide-open, cum-dripping holes.

Soon thereafter the guys dressed and left, each getting a big kiss from Susan.

"Maybe we can do this again?" Steve asked. Or maybe it was Jerry. Who cared, Susan thought. He had fucked her ass soooo good! As Ted and a sore Susan were dressing to leave, Greg poked his head back in the door and said "My folks will be out of town next week if you guys want to come over."

Ted said, "Ah, well, maybe -"

"You bet!" Susan corrected him. "But only invite Paul over."

"Why?" Greg asked.

"I've been thinking. I'd like you two to do something to me that I've always wanted to try."

"What?" both Ted and Greg asked in unison.

"I'd like you boys to double penetrate my pussy."

"Yeah!" Greg replied. "I'll e-mail you for what time on Saturday. See ya slut!"

"Bye stud!" Susan called back.

Then turning to Ted, Susan smiled and asked. "Did you like seeing mommy getting fucked by all your friends?" He didn't answer. "Well, did you?" Susan demanded.

"Yes," Ted replied meekly.

"Yes what?" she snapped.

"Yes! I really like seeing all my friends fuck my mom!"

"Good boy! You're such a good son, Teddy. Mommy will keep fucking all your friends for as long as she wants, to. Mommy's really enjoying all your big-dicked young friends. I think from now on I'm gonna have to keep fucking all your friends. And when they get too old, we'll have to find more young friends, so mommy can keep fucking your friends for years to come! Doesn't that sound good?"

And Ted got hard yet again.

CHAPTER 11

By the following Friday, Roger was so horny for his mom's cunt, since they hadn't fucked in a couple of weeks. Susan had finally recovered from the fabulous fuck Greg had arranged for her the previous Saturday, and she couldn't wait for this Saturday night when she and Ted were going to Greg's since his folks were gone for the weekend. Susan came into Roger's room Friday evening and found her son sitting up in bed stroking his hard cock.

"Sorry I'm late," Susan said. "I was on the computer." As Susan dropped to her knees, she bent over to take her son's cock in her mouth. Roger held his mom's head as she licked up and down his shaft, sucking his cockhead and then deep-throating him. Susan then pulled up slowly, her saliva trickling down to Roger's pubes and balls.

"Oh man," Roger moaned. "You suck cock good, mom." Susan moaned around the cockhead only to repeat the deep-throating technique that her son loved. "Ah, man, yeah" Roger groaned. "You sure are inspired tonight!" Again his mom moaned around the cockhead thinking about the double fuck she would receive from her son's friends the following night. Finally Roger could hold out no longer. Susan took his cockhead in her mouth and began fisting his slicked-up shaft, faster, faster, faster.

"Ahh! Ahh! Oh yeah!" Roger cried as he shot his load down his mom's throat. "Fuck that was good," Roger said after Susan took his cock from her mouth to lick him clean. "I can't wait for tomorrow to get that again."

"Tomorrow?" Susan thought. "Oh shit!" In all the excitement over Saturday night, Susan forgot that she fucked Roger every Saturday. But she didn't want herself too fucked-out and sore. Greg and Paul were both going to fuck her cunt. At the same time!

"Um, honey," Susan managed to say. "I forgot about tomorrow."

"What?" Roger asked.

"I've got some things to do off and on all day and -"

"Aw fuck, mom! Come on! You promised!"

"I know, I know! Listen, I'll make it up to you -"

"Yeah right!"

"I will."

"Just forget it," Roger groaned, turning away from her. Susan, feeling guilty, stood up and kissed her son's cheek. "I'm sorry," she said. "I promise. I WILL make it up to you." And with that she left his room.

The next day, Roger startled Ted when he asked to go into work with him. Ted knew all about the argument last night, and let his angry son accompany him. That evening, Susan and Ted again dressed like they were going to go out. Roger didn't say a word this time, as he watched a ballgame on TV. Still feeling guilty, Susan said nothing but Ted spoke up saying, "Uh Roger, we'll be back in a few hours." And they walked out.

"They're so fucked up," Roger thought. Once their car drove off, Roger decided to call Greg to see what was happening. "Uh, I can't man," Greg informed him. "I've got a chick coming over."

"Yeah who?" Roger asked. "It's just someone that I met. Look she's gonna be over any minute so I gotta split," Greg said hanging up.

Roger then tried Paul but he had just left. "You know when he'll be back?" Roger asked Paul's mom.

"I don't know sweetie, I'm sorry. I think he said something about going out with Greg but that's all I know."

"What the fuck?" Roger thought as he hung up. As the minutes past Roger thought and thought. "Greg's gonna fuck some girl tonight with Paul and they're not inviting me? The bastards!" Roger mulled angrily until he thought that maybe he could check it out. Greg didn't live too far, less than a mile away. His house was big. Maybe Roger could see who they were doing. You know, just wander around the outside and hopefully peek through a window or something. Then Roger left the house and walked to Greg's. When he got there he noticed a familiar car in the driveway. "What the fuck is this?" Roger thought. What were his parents doing here? Then his mind drifted back many weeks earlier when his mom mentioned something about fucking his friends; for his father. "They're BOTH in there. With Greg and Paul!" Roger's head screamed. That's the "chick" Greg is fucking! That's the 'older woman' Paul is fucking! Oh my god!" Roger was angry and wanted to cry. He didn't know what to do. He couldn't storm in, but ran around the house looking for a window. He needed to see for himself. He entered the back yard and noticed the sliding back door. He could see light from the living room and as he got closer, in the darkness, Roger took a peak inside. His eyes opened wide, and his mouth fell open.

There on the couch was his father, Ted, naked and playing with himself, while on the carpeted floor, Greg was lying down with his mom straddling him, while holding Greg's shoulders. Meanwhile, Paul was behind her up-turned ass, moving to and fro. Roger's world began crashing all around him. He watched as his friends fucked his own mom. In and out, in and out, up and down, up and down, thrusting their huge young pricks in and out of her as Susan cried out for more. His mom was squealing in a way he'd never heard a woman do before, certainly not with him. Susan moaned and cried in pleasure, accentuated with lots of "Ow, ow ows!' but for her it was all worth it!

Then Roger noticed something peculiar. Fucking his mom from behind, Paul took a couple of fingers and shoved them in her ass. "What the fuck!" Roger thought. "If his fingers are in her ass, then where's his cock? No fucking way!" Total way! Roger was amazed watching his whorish, slut mom getting double penetrated in her PUSSY! And Roger knew just how well-hung his friends were, too. Both studs continued to work their cocks as far up Susan's cunt as they could, destroying her for all time. Roger noticed his dad start shooting his cum into a glass so as not to get it on the carpet. Greg and Paul, sweating, grunting, groaning calling Susan a "bitch," a "whore," an "older woman slut," continued pounding their pricks in and out of

her dripping cunt. And Roger noticed his mom: sweaty, mouth ajar, licking her lips, crying in pleasure, her eyes glazed, cumming yet again. She was fucking loving it!

Roger backed away. It was all he could handle. Walking faster, he started to jog and then broke into a run. How could his mom do all this? Why was his dad so perverted? And why, Roger wondered in the dark of night, was his own cock so fucking hard.

CHAPTER 12

Roger ran into the house, angry, crying at what his mom was doing with his friends. Those bastards! Fucking her cunt at the same time! And his wimp dad, just sitting their whacking off to it. Roger in anger, got out of his clothes but couldn't get the visions of the double pussy penetration out of his mind. His breathing increased as he saw his whore mom in such a state of ecstasy, calling out to his friends to give it all to her. Watching the movie in his mind, Roger uncontrollably started playing with his rock hard cock and the closer they all got to cumming, so did he. When he heard his mom crying out in orgasm yet again, Roger shot his load all over the floor. "Fucking bitch," Roger groaned. He loved it, too. But hated them all.

By the time Susan and Ted got home, Roger was already fast asleep having polished off one of their bottles of scotch. The next day, after getting over his hang-over, Roger was silent, not talking to anyone. Ted and Susan noticed but didn't say anything. She figured he was still sore from breaking their date. She was sore, period. That evening, Susan went to Roger's room to give him his nightly blowjob.

"Go away," Roger said.

"Why?" Susan asked. "Look, sweetie, I'm really sorry about last night."

"No your not!" Roger replied. "I saw everything, you fucking whore!" Susan was silent and quickly turned white with fear. "My own fucking friends, you bitch! Just get out! I don't wanna fucking touch you! Get OUT!"

Susan, shaking and starting to cry, backed out and went down the hall to her room. Ted was already there. "What the hell happened?" he asked. Crying, Susan said, "He knows. He saw everything." Ted was shocked. How? What? It didn't matter. Except that now everything was beyond fucked-up.

From that moment, things changed dramatically. Susan e-mailed Greg: "Roger found out. Can't do this anymore. Don't contact me." Roger immediately broke up with his friends who avoided him, as well. Roger spent less and less time at home, and wouldn't even go near Ted's place of business. He got himself a girlfriend just to have someone and somewhere to go. Susan tried to talk to him but he wouldn't respond. She felt guilty, Ted felt guilty, and both turned on each other as well. Why did HE have to start it all with his sick fantasies? Why did SHE insist on doing the kid's friends? Thankfully, the school year ended and Roger graduated. He spent the summer preparing to go off to college, and unfortunately for all concerned, it was the best remedy. Roger would be away from home for the better part of the next four years. Guilt and anger would linger, but also a chance to heal somewhat. Out of sight out of mind.

For Susan, once Roger had gone, reality set in. His friend's were gone, too. No one was around and Susan, who hadn't been laid in months once again took out her black vibrator, plunging it into her horny, aching cunt. The only thing more powerful than her guilt was her needs. After thrusting the fake cock in and out of her wet pussy for seemingly the millionth time, Susan pulled it out and thought, "Fuck it! I don't care anymore. I'm gonna do what I want. What I NEED! Fuck everyone!"

That night she called her friend Donna. "Donna, tell me, what are you doing this weekend?"

"I've got my boys coming over. Why?"

"You want company?"

"Susie, are you fucking serious?"

"Yes. God Donna, I've always wanted to do this! I envy you so much!"

"Why didn't you ever tell me?" Then Susan informed Donna about her black vibrator and that the timing was finally right. Donna promised her an evening she'd never forget. "This is just the beginning Susie-girl. Come Saturday night, you're a changed woman."

Susan informed Ted. She was going to Donna's. She was gonna try a black cock. He wasn't invited. From now on he could just read his sex-stories and whack off. Late Saturday night, Susan came home, telling Ted how great Tyrone and E.J. were; how big their cocks were and that they were all going to do it again the next weekend. In their own house! In their own bed!

"This is the way it's gonna be from now on, Ted," Susan informed him. The following Saturday, Ted watched, and jacked-off to the sight of his little blond wife and her buxom brunette friend getting fucked by two nineteen year-old black studs with nearly ten inches apiece. At one point, Tyrone was fucking Susan on the bed while she tried stuffing her mouth with E.J.s fat black prick. Just then Donna came over to Ted who was sitting naked on a chair, watching and masturbating. Donna crouched down to take his little dick in her mouth. "Look at her, Ted," Donna said between licks. "She loves it." Susan was in ecstasy, getting the kind of fuck she'd always wanted. "Psst Ted," Donna whispered over the sound of Susan's cries. "She's not going back. She's gonna whore, now. Like me!" Then Ted shot off into Donna's mouth. To top it off, when Tyrone and E.J left, after depositing a gallon of cum into both Donna and Susan, Donna snapped, "Come here Ted! Go eat your wife!"

"Yeah, come here, Teddy!" Susan said. "This is what you're good for." Lying back in bed, Susan spread her legs where her obscenely wide-open cunt was red, sore and leaking cum. "Do it, Ted!" she snapped. "Eat me!" Once Ted started licking, Donna said "That's a good bitch." Ted kept eating the black-man cum out of his wife's cunt until she lifted herself to expose her massively opened, leaking asshole. "There, too!" Susan snapped, as Ted rimmed her as well. "I think we're training him real good, Donna, Susan said. Now, Teddy, eat Donna, too." He did.

By the time Roger was back home the following summer, his parents were deep into the scene. One Saturday night, Roger had gone out and by the time he returned his folks still weren't home. He went to bed and soon thereafter, Ted and Susan got home. Looking out his window, he saw his folks heading for the door, with his mom in a little halter top, real tiny shorts, and heels. "What the fuck," Roger thought. She and Donna had been at a party with five young black studs. When they were in their bedroom, Roger overheard his mom talking strangely. Curiously, Roger went to investigate. Standing by the closed door, he listened.

"Oooh yeah, Teddy. You service me so good. You like eating black cum, dontcha! Huh? Dontcha?"

"Um, hmm," he moaned lapping his wife. "How would you like it if I had a black baby? Would you like that Teddy? Hmm? I want a black baby Ted! Don't you want me to have one, too?"

"Um, hmm." came the reply. "They're fucking sick," Roger thought, and went to his room.

Roger eventually graduated college and married his college sweetheart. His relationship with his parents would always remain strained. His mom never did get pregnant, that was just a game they shared, but she spent years thereafter prowling with Donna, doing young black men regularly. Ted never got near her cunt again except to eat it. Roger tried to settle down and live a "normal" life. Ten years and two kids later, all was great.

Then Roger came home from work early one day and heard noises coming from his bedroom. Unmistakable noises. Nervously he poked his head around to find his wife of twelve years, on the bed, on her hands and knees, and behind her was the neighbor's son, the starting quarterback on the high school football team, fucking his wife! Roger was shocked, and his knees grew weak.

Not again! Roger stood unmoving watching the handsome, weel-built teen star fuck his own wife and in his own bed! And she was loving it! Crying out for it harder and faster! When the kid finally came, he pulled his cock out of her cunt. It was massive! And still hard! Then the stud began working his slick teen schlong into his wife's ass.

"Ooooh yeeaahh!" she cried. "I love your big, fat cock up my ass! Fuck me!" The young man fucked the older woman's asshole as Roger just watched from around the corner. Memories roared back to life for Roger. It was all too much. "Oooohh, I love it when you fuck my ass!" his wife cried. As the young man filled her bowels with cum, he pulled his massive member out. Roger's wife collapsed on the bed as the stud rested beside her. Roger quickly backed away and left.

Driving away Roger was still in shock. They've fucked before! His wife was fucking the boy next door! Roger couldn't get the vision out of his head! The huge cock fucking her cunt, fucking her ass! Then Roger painfully noticed his cock was rock hard! And he liked it, too! He knew he wanted to see them do it again! And again! And again!

THE END

view adult content, you must exit now. <u>*Adults Only*</u>*.*

Share your thoughts with us.
Take a moment to tell us how we're doing.   Your feedback really matters.

You can reach us by:
Email: <u>*my777books@yahoo.com*</u>

Search for other titles by Sophie MacDonald.

www.ingramcontent.com/pod-product-compliance
Lightning Source LLC
LaVergne TN
LVHW011255200326
834410LV00006B/271